Jordan the Jellyfish

A Chesapeake Bay Adventure

Story inspired by true events

By Cindy Freland

This book is dedicated to my beautiful daughters,

Alyssa and Andrea Bean

Thanks for all the encouragement, love and laughter. I love you!

This book is also dedicated to the Chesapeake Bay. Please help save this national treasure. 5% of the proceeds go to the Chesapeake Bay Foundation.

CHESAPEAKE BAY FOUNDATION
Saving a National Treasure

5% of the proceeds from the sale of this book go to the Chesapeake Bay Foundation.

Chesapeake Bay Foundation
Vision

The Chesapeake Bay is a national treasure. America's largest estuary is worth more than one trillion dollars, home to 17 million people, and populated with iconic wildlife. But despite some recent signs of improvement, the Bay is still a system dangerously out of balance. Poor water quality is threatening our local rivers, streams, and the Bay; endangering the health of thousands of species of plants and animals; putting human health at risk; and deflating our region's economy. The Chesapeake Bay Foundation is committed to making the Bay and its rivers and streams healthy again. And, with the help of dedicated members, we work across the six-state Chesapeake Bay watershed to do just that. Our vision is a restored Bay with healthy rivers and clean water; sustainable populations of crabs, fish, and oysters; thriving water-based and agricultural economies; and a legacy of success for our children and grandchildren.

Learn more about the foundation on the website at http://www.cbf.org.

Author:
Cindy Freland

Cindy Freland's inspiration comes from her love of children and animals. Most of her children's books are based on true events. She founded Maryland Secretarial Services, Inc. in 1997. She has won three business awards and teaches business workshops at two local community colleges, a senior center and two chamber of commerce offices. She offers word processing, data entry, desktop publishing and transcription to businesses of all sizes, government agencies, non-profit organizations and individuals throughout the United States. Her passion is teaching workshops, designing and managing Facebook pages and helping authors get their books on Amazon. She has written many business books, including one on Facebook for business, "Easy Guide to Your Facebook Business Page," and several children's books. You can find her books on Amazon, at http://www. amazon.com. Freland lives in Bowie, Maryland with her family and puppy, Juno.

Illustrator:
Jon C. Munson II

Jon C. Munson II is a digital artist and photographer. He also works with his parents supporting their lawn maintenance service, NaturaLawn of America. He enjoys spiritual pursuits, sailing, bowling, music, native instruments (Native American flute & drums), Legos, R/C trains, and many other interests. He lives in Bowie, Maryland, with his family. See examples of his art and photography below, and also by visiting http://jon-munson-ii. artistwebsites.com.

Jellyfish: Friend or Foe?

For most residents of Maryland, thoughts of jellyfish bring terror to otherwise fun beach adventures. But despite its scary character, jellyfish play an important role in the Chesapeake Bay ecosystem. Some jellyfish even help the bay's smaller animals from growing too large in numbers.

During the summer, Sea Nettles thrive around the bay, because of the low salt content. Their tentacles can grow up to six feet long. The tentacles are what cause the feared sting to swimmers.

While nettles are mostly known for the stinging pain they cause to swimmers, these animals are also important because they eat comb jellies. Comb jellies eat fish and oyster larvae in the bay, making sea nettles a friend of many of the bay's fish species and a very dear friend of the watermen.

Alyssa and Andrea were at Sandy Point State Park in Maryland with their mom. It was July 19 and Andrea's birthday.

They could see the Chesapeake Bay Bridge in the distance.

The sand was scorching hot as they walked with the blue and white cooler and green and purple striped chairs. They were wearing sandals but the hot sand was getting under their feet as they walked, causing them to leave the cooler and the chairs behind so they could run to the water.

The Chesapeake Bay Bridge opened in 1952, with a length of over four miles, it was the world's longest over-water steel structure at the time. The parallel span was added in 1973. The bridge connects the rural Eastern Shore with the urban Western Shore of Maryland. Its average DAILY traffic is 61,000 cars.

The water cooled their feet enough for them to move the stuff a little closer with not-so-hot feet. They had to stop three times to cool their feet before they were able to get all their stuff to the perfect spot on the beach.

Once they found the perfect spot, they put down their stuff and the girls ran off into the water. Kids were playing with huge tubes and inflated alligators. Oops, there go a pair of pink flip flops into the water. Two kids were burying a man in the sand so only his head was showing. They were all laughing and happy.

Sandy Point State Park is open year round. This 786-acre park is located along the Northwestern shore of the scenic Chesapeake Bay.

The girls played for hours in the water but now it was time for lunch. "Time for lunch, girls," Alyssa and Andrea's mom yelled. The girls ran out of the water and onto the hot sand again. "Mmm, yummy, I'm hungry," said Alyssa. "Me too," said Andrea. They had chicken salad on rolls, watermelon, all cut up with the seeds removed, and potato chips for lunch with water to drink. After they finished eating, they waited 15 minutes so they wouldn't get cramps. Then they ran back into the water to play again.

A dog was playing in the water and having fun with the kids. The sun was shining, there was a slight breeze, and it wasn't too hot. It was a perfect day. The girls were having a great time in the water until, AHHHHHHHH!

There was a loud scream. Andrea was screaming and crying. A huge jellyfish was hanging out of Andrea's swim suit and stinging her leg. Her mom ran over to her and washed off the jellyfish. But Andrea was still crying from the pain. The jellyfish swam away.

Andrea was lucky this time as most jellyfish stings are not harmful. She will just be uncomfortable and her leg will feel like the combination of a bee sting and bad sunburn.

> *There are many types of Jellyfish. The most common in the Chesapeake Bay is the Sea Nettle. Jellyfish leave needle-like stingers, called nematocysts, in their prey. The stingers are in the tentacles and they can inject millions of nematocysts filled with venom, or poison, into the skin.*

Jordan, the jellyfish, or sea nettle, was very sad. She had accidentally stung a human girl. She would never do that on purpose. Jordan wanted to get home as quickly as possible. She got lost with all the commotion at the beach. Jordan's home was near Mayo Beach, which was a long way from Sandy Point. But which way should she go?

Which of these animals in the Chesapeake Bay could help Jordan find her way home? Since Jordan was an underwater creature, maybe it would be another underwater creature, like a crab, fish, clam or another jellyfish.

Jordan swam in the direction she thought was the way. But she wasn't sure. What if she swam and swam for days and never found her way home? Would she have to make a new home for herself? She would never see her family or her friends again.

> *The Chesapeake Bay is 200 miles from Havre de Grace, Maryland to Norfolk, Virginia. It is the home for many animals, including, jellyfish, blue crabs, oysters, clams, striped bass, turtles, frogs, bald eagles and ospreys.*

Would she have to make new friends? What if she couldn't find her favorite foods? Would she have to learn to eat something else?

Jordan swam for a while and the water seemed warmer. The water was so beautiful and clean here.

Jordan saw lots of oysters. She heard they clean the bay and she was thankful for their help. Oscar the Oyster was swimming by but he didn't have time to chat with Jordan.

There were schools of fish and crabs were swimming on the bottom of the bay. What a nice place to live if she couldn't find her way home.

Then she saw something shining below her. She swam lower to see what it was. Could it be something to help her find her way home? She swam closer. Then she was scared. What if this was something that would hurt her?

> *The eastern oyster is one of the most popular creatures in the Chesapeake Bay. Oysters were one of the most valuable harvests for over 100 years. The over-harvesting, disease, and poor water quality has caused a severe decline in their numbers throughout the Bay. There are many non-profit groups to help increase the number of oysters.*

What if it was another human? But she was curious so she swam closer. Then she noticed there was more than one. There were thousands of tiny, shiny fish. It was a school of bay anchovies and they were eating fish larvae.

Even though Jordan was still scared, she wanted to find out if the anchovies could help her. So she asked the largest fish if he knew the direction of Mayo Beach. The anchovy said his name was Arthur and Jordan introduced herself. Arthur pointed to the direction he thought it was and it was the same direction that Jordan was swimming. So she was happy about that. Jordan enjoyed swimming with the anchovies for a while.

Also known as the rockfish or striper, the striped bass is a large predatory fish with dark stripes running across its metallic sides. It lives throughout the Chesapeake Bay year round.

"Why do your tentacles look so different Arthur?" asked Jordan. "These are fins. They help me swim," said Arthur.

Then Jordan saw the anchovies swimming away very quickly. She was very scared. What could make them swim so quickly? Arthur was scared too. Arthur said he saw a huge striped bass. He had seen this bass eat other anchovies and he didn't want any part of it. So Arthur told Jordan to follow him to a tiny crack in a cave. Arthur fit into the cave but Jordan was too big.

Arthur hid in the cave as the other anchovies swam away in fright. The bass wasn't being nice to her new friend, Arthur. Jordan just had to help him. But how could she help? Then Jordan had an idea. She swam away from the cave as fast as she could and the bass followed her. Will the bass be mean to her too? Arthur was able to swim away, unharmed and he found his school. The bass was getting so close to her and Jordan was very scared.

> *The bay anchovy is the most common and important fish in the Chesapeake Bay. It eats plankton and is a major food for large fish, making it a key species in the Bay's ecosystem.*

Then, all of a sudden, there was a huge SPLASH! The bass swam away and Jordan was safe again. A woman was fishing from the pier near the Chesapeake Bay Bridge. Her foot got tangled in fishing line and she was barefoot. She stepped on a fishhook and fell into the water.

Jordan felt badly about stinging the little girl at the beach so she wanted to help. As Jordan swam closer, she noticed the woman was swimming AWAY!

Maybe the woman heard that jellyfish sting humans. Jordan didn't want to scare her or sting her but she wanted to help. Jordan just kept swimming towards her and the woman just kept swimming closer to the beach.

The woman climbed onto the rocks near the bridge to rest. Jordan could hear men yelling from the bridge to the woman, saying they were coming down to help her. The woman could walk up the hill with their assistance. Jordan thought she had made another friend. But the woman needed medical help and she needed to get back to her family.

The watermen of the Chesapeake Bay are kept busy all year. They catch eels, yellow perch, catfish, and clams in the spring, blue crabs in the summer, oysters in the fall, striped bass and perch in the winter. The watermen supply the seafood that Maryland residents eat.

FAMILY! Jordan's family must be worried sick. She continued on her journey to find her home. But which direction should she go now? She got lost when the bass was chasing her. She spotted the school of anchovies and her new friend, Arthur, so she knew this was the right way.

Jordan started getting very hungry. At home she would eat comb jellies and other creatures. But could she find them here, in this strange place?

Jordan found some comb jellies to eat. While she was enjoying her meal, she watched a school of colorful fish swimming. They reminded her of when she raced with friends near her home.

Then Jordan felt something suddenly move under her. She was being gently lifted into a net with lots of other fish. Then she was placed on the deck of a waterman's boat.

How was she supposed to get back into the water? Then she heard a boy laughing and the sound got LOUDER and LOUDER. There was a stomping sound on the deck. The boy was chasing his dog towards her and the other fish that were caught in the net. A man was yelling, "Stop, don't run Kyle," but it was too late. The boy slipped on the wet deck and pushed the net full of fish, including Jordan, back into the water. Whew! Jordan was happy again.

The fish and Jordan were still entangled in the net. How could they get out? Jordan noticed the dog was in the water too. The people on the boat were yelling for the dog, but the dog had no way to get back on the boat.

The man jumped into the water to rescue the dog. But before the man could get him, the dog panicked and cut a hole in the net with his claws. All the fish, including Jordan, escaped and swam away in fright. The man got the dog safely back on the boat.

Jordan needed to find help so she could get home. But maybe the boat had helped her after all. Maybe the boat got her closer to her home near Mayo Beach.

She looked for the Chesapeake Bay Bridge to see if she was still close to it. But to her surprise, it was nowhere in sight. She must be getting closer to her home. She just knew it.

Comb jellies eat the fish larvae and small shrimp that are caught by the Chesapeake Bay Watermen when the fish and shrimp grow larger.

It was getting dark and Jordan was tired. She could see the moon shining through the water. She had a very rough day. She stung a girl, got lost, made a friend, was chased by a striped bass, helped a woman, was caught in a net and then she was rescued by a dog.

What else was going to happen before she found her way home? She couldn't think about that right now. If she was going to find her way home, she needed to rest. But where would she be safe for the night?

What is that huge shadow? It was getting BIGGER and BIGGER! It was a turtle and it was getting very close to Jordan.

Jordan was very scared again but she wanted to be brave. She swam as fast as she could to get away from the turtle. She swam in and out of the port holes of an old boat that looked like it had been there forever. She swam what seemed like a very long way and the turtle was close behind her the whole time.

The Atlantic Loggerhead is a sea turtle who enjoys eating jellyfish, sponges, squid, fish, barnacles and sea grasses. It is the most common sea turtle in the Chesapeake Bay.

There were lots of treasures on the boat but Jordan didn't have time to stop and look. She was too busy trying to get away from the turtle.

Then she remembered Arthur hiding in a crack in a cave when the bass was chasing them. She looked for a cave to hide. Jordan remembered arguing with her brother that morning and she felt sad. She missed her family.

Curtis, the blue crab, was watching Jordan being chased by the turtle and he wanted to help her.

Curtis swam close to the turtle, stopped in front of him so the turtle could see him and then Curtis opened his claws to scare the turtle.

But Curtis didn't have to do anything. The turtle was scared and swam away quickly. Whew! Curtis saved Jordan.

"Wow! That was close. My name is Curtis. Who are you and what were you looking for?" said Curtis. "Thanks so much for helping me Curtis. My name is Jordan and I am trying to find my way home to Mayo Beach. I am tired and I was trying to find a place to rest for the night. Will you please help me?" said Jordan.

The blue crab is the Maryland state crustacean. In 2009, there were 223 million adults and they increased to 753 million in 2012 in the Chesapeake Bay. There were only 300 million in 2013, the lowest number in five years. The largest blue crab caught in the Chesapeake Bay was 10.72 inches and weighed 1.1 pounds.

"I sleep in the mud at the bottom of the bay. You are welcome to stay with me," said Curtis. "I don't sleep in the mud but I would feel safer if I rested near you," said Jordan.

"How did you get lost?" said Curtis. "I was arguing with my brother this morning and he pushed me. I was caught in the current and I drifted away. I even stung a little girl at the beach today. I feel so badly about hurting her," said Jordan.

> *More than 2,700 types of plants grow throughout the Chesapeake Bay watershed. Plants grow from forests to the shoreline and help keep the air and water clean. Plants also provide habitats for many mammals, birds and fish.*

"Don't worry. Sea nettle stings aren't dangerous. The little girl was uncomfortable for a few hours but she is probably fine now," said Curtis. "I'm glad she will be okay," said Jordan.

"Why do your tentacles look so different Curtis?" asked Jordan. "These aren't tentacles. They are claws. I use them to open clam shells," said Curtis. "And scare away huge turtles," Jordan said with a smile.

As Jordan rested while Curtis snuggled into the mud to sleep, she remembered the argument with her brother that morning. They argued about who had the longest tentacles, he or Jordan. "What a stupid thing to argue over," she thought to herself. She also thought that you shouldn't argue with loved ones. Sure, there will be disagreements and different opinions, but everyone is entitled to their choices.

Now she didn't know if she would ever get home.

Jordan didn't sleep very well but she rested near Curtis all night and she felt safe. The morning brought thoughts of new adventures.

Would she meet some new friends to help her? Would she finally find her way home today?

Jordan missed her dad the most. He was strong and kind. Her dad helped her learn to hunt and make a nest. She missed her mom and her brother too. Jordan had a pet ghost anemone, named Angel. Angel kept Jordan calm and taught Jordan to be helpful to her family.

Curtis woke up and told Jordan that it was time to leave. She needed to find her way home today. The longer she was gone, the more chance there was that she would get hurt or never find her way home.

But first Curtis and Jordan wanted a little fun. They raced to the pier and back. Then she said "goodbye" to Curtis and thanked him for his help. The sun was shining and Jordan could hear people laughing and splashing in the water. She must be near a beach. But could it be Mayo Beach? Nothing looked familiar so she knew it couldn't be her home.

But what Jordan didn't know was that it was Mayo Beach. Her home was on the other side of the bay. She finally made it there.

Jordan swam closer to the pier where people were catching crabs. She wanted to see if anything looked familiar or if she could get some help.

Two children and a man were crabbing with strings. They had already caught several large blue crabs. The crabs were alive in an orange bucket on the pier. The boy threw the string into the water to catch another crab.

A large crab was tugging on the string. The boy lifted the string to catch the crab in his net. OH, NO! Curtis was on the end of the string!

Jordan had to help her friend. She panicked and swam closer to the pier. But how could she help him? She couldn't get out of the water or she would dry up. Maybe David the duck could help. But David was with his family and didn't want to be disturbed.

> *The osprey, also known as the fish hawk, is a large bird of prey with a distinctive brown and white pattern. It visits the shorelines, rivers and marshes of the Chesapeake Bay, from spring through late summer. They mostly feed on medium-sized fish.*

Then she saw a huge shadow moving on the pier. Overhead was a huge osprey. It was Olivia and she was looking for a meal and a blue crab was just what she wanted to bring home to her family. But Olivia and Curtis were friends.

MAYO
BEACH

Curtis helped her a long time ago and Olivia never forgot. So Olivia flew in closer and closer. She was able to get close enough to the boy so he was scared and dropped the string. Curtis dropped into the water and escaped.

> **The largest source of pollution to the Bay comes from agricultural runoff, which contributes roughly 40 percent of the nitrogen.**

Olivia skimmed the water and caught a fish. She went back to her nest on the post in the bay. She had two hungry babies waiting for their meal.

But Jordan still didn't know how to get home. Curtis swam over to the post where Olivia was feeding her babies. "Olivia, do you know where Mayo Beach is?" asked Curtis.

Olivia looked around and saw a sign in the sand. It read, "Mayo Beach." "There it is, right there Curtis," she said. Curtis was so excited to finally help Jordan get home. He thanked Olivia for helping and tried to find Jordan to tell her.

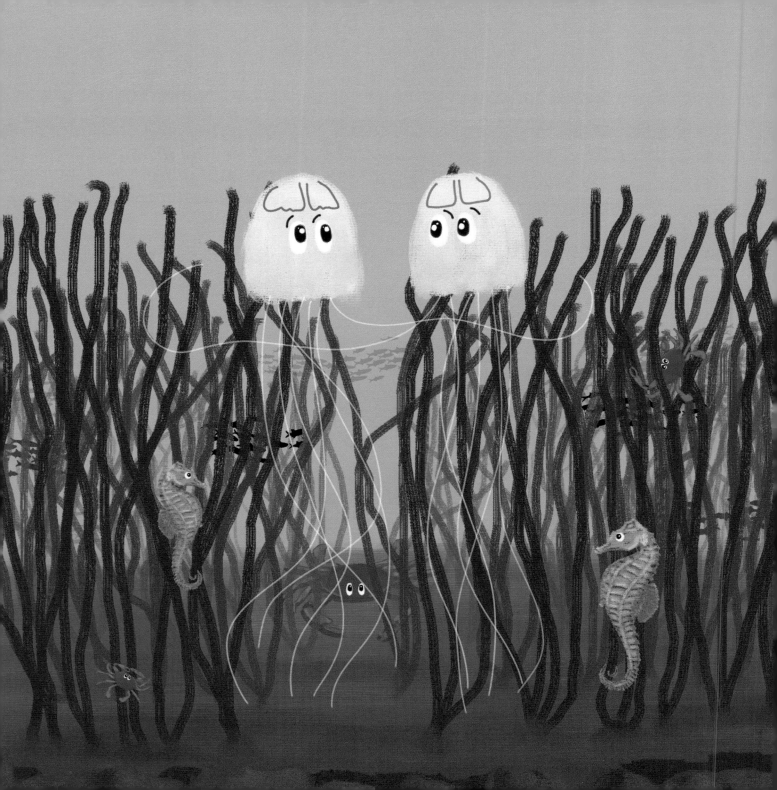

But Jordan had already found her way home. Her brother, Jeremy, saw the commotion between the crab and the osprey and he wanted to check it out. He saw Jordan watching in the water.

Jeremy quickly swam to Jordan. "Jeremy!" Jordan screamed with happiness. Jordan was so happy to see her brother again and she gave him a big hug. Jeremy said he was sorry for arguing and pushing her and he would try to never do that again.

Mayo Beach Park sits at the mouth of the Chesapeake Bay and the South River in Anne Arundel County, Maryland. The park is not open to the general public and is only available by permit. It is a gorgeous location for weddings, receptions, cultural exhibits, company picnics and family reunions.

Jeremy told Jordan that their mom had dinner ready so they needed to get back home quickly. Jordan said, "Let's go, I'm starving." "You are always hungry Jordan," said Jeremy. "Well, I am a growing jellyfish," Jordan said with a giggle.

She remembered that Curtis helped her so she wanted to say goodbye to him. But he had already seen that Jordan was home so he went home too.

Curtis lived with his family in a gorgeous part of Mayo Beach. He enjoyed helping the creatures of the Bay and hearing music play during weddings at the beach.

Curtis and Jordan will always be friends and now they were neighbors. They will see each other again very soon.

The ghost anemone is a jelly-like invertebrate with a flat, rounded base and stinging tentacles. It attaches itself to pilings, reefs, rocks and other hard surfaces throughout the Chesapeake Bay. It is related to sea nettles.

Jordan and Jeremy went home. Her parents were so happy that Jordan was back safely. Jordan told her family all about her Chesapeake Bay adventure and how her friends, Arthur the Anchovy, Curtis the Crab and Olivia the Osprey helped her. Angel was extra happy to see her because Angel wanted to be fed and Jordan was the only one who could find Angel's favorite treat.

DO NOT READ ALOUD:
FOR PARENTS

There are millions of children that get lost or kidnapped every day. Please, please watch your children.

If you must leave them with someone, be sure you leave them with someone you trust. Even family members and friends have been known to be kidnappers and abusers.

Children like to hide and because they don't know the dangers, they take risks and they are very trusting. YOU need to teach them the dangers.

WHAT IF YOU GET LOST

Jordan got lost but she found her home again with the help of some friends. Visiting new places is a lot of fun. But what happens when you get lost? Getting lost in an unknown place is scary at any age. What should you do if you get lost? Here are a few tips:

1.   **Get Safe:** Get to a safe place. For example: If you are in the street, first look both ways for cars and then walk slowly and carefully to the sidewalk.

2.   **Stand Up:** Stand up straight and tall and call out the adult's names. They may be closer than you think and hear you.

3.   **Listen:** The adults might be calling your name. So listen for someone calling you. If you hear them, walk in the direction of their voice. Watch for cars and holes in the sidewalk.

4.   **Go Back:** Try to safely go back to the place where you last saw the adults. Be sure to look both ways before crossing any streets.

5.   **Ask Adult:** If you cannot find the adults you came with, try to find an adult and ask them for help.

PLEASE HELP THE CHESAPEAKE BAY

The Chesapeake Bay is a gorgeous place to live, work and play. Check the website at http://www.cfb.org for more information on what you can do to help.

What can you do to help?
1. Become a member of the Chesapeake Bay Foundation and other Bay organizations.

2. Volunteer to help clean the Bay.

3. Join the Chesapeake Bay Action Network and speak out for the Bay!

4. Check the education section if you are a teacher. There are professional development initiatives, student education programs and more.

5. Throw trash in trash cans or take it with you.

6. Never throw anything into the Bay.

7. Never harm animals or dig up plants.

8. Help spread the word about the Bay.

9. Swim and fish in designated areas.

FACTS ABOUT JELLYFISH

A jellyfish sting feels like a bee sting and sunburn at the same time. Jellyfish usually are quite common in the Chesapeake Bay in July and August. When you get a sting, the jellyfish leaves thousands of very tiny stingers that continue pumping poison into your skin. The best thing to do when there is a jellyfish sting is to wash it off with bay water. Fresh water may cause the stingers to fire. Then rinse the skin with vinegar, if you have it.

Be sure to call an ambulance if someone has been stung and they are having trouble breathing, they have a swollen tongue or lips, they have bad pain or they were stung on the eye or mouth.

To avoid getting stung by jellyfish, ask the attendant at the beach gate if there are many jellyfish in the water. Look for a purple flag on the beach, which means that there is dangerous marine life in the water and look for nets in the water that help keep marine life out of the swimming area. A lifeguard on the beach will help too. Bring a small container of vinegar with you, just in case of a sting.

Jellyfish are not made of jelly and they are not fish. They live in oceans all over the world and they have lived for 700 million years, even longer than the dinosaurs. Jellyfish are not only hazardous in the water but watch out for them on the shore. They might look dried out but they can still sting you.

BOOKS WRITTEN BY CINDY FRELAND

You will find books written by Cindy Freland on Amazon.com:

Pond Adventures with Chippy
Pond Adventures with Aragon
Felix and the Purple Giant
Easy Guide to Your Facebook Business Page
Get a Job! Your Resume and Interview Guide
Monkey Farts: A Guide to Selling Your Handmade Crafts and Direct Sales Products
Easy and Free Self-Publishing: A Guide to Getting Your Book in Print and Kindle on Amazon
An American Virtual Assistant: The "Good, Bad and Ugly of Owning a Business Support Service
You Might Be Surprised: Marketing Ideas to Help Grow Your Business
Who Ate All The Apples? Lessons from my Brother
Mud Pies
No More Excuses: How to start a profitable business from your home on a shoestring budget